THE EMPLOYEES

Olga Ravn

THE EMPLOYEES

a workplace novel of the 22nd century

translated from the Danish
by Martin Aitken

A NEW DIRECTIONS BOOK

Originally published in Danish as *De ansatte*.
Published by agreement with Gyldendal Group Agency.

This translation was first published in the United Kingdom by Lolli Editions
in 2020. It was made possible through the generous support
of the Danish Arts Foundation and the Fondation Jan Michalski.

First published clothbound by New Directions in 2022
and as New Directions Paperbook 1548 (ISBN 978-0-8112-3482-5) in 2023
Manufactured in the United States of America
Design by Erik Rieselbach

Library of Congress Cataloging-in-Publication Data
Names: Ravn, Olga, author. | Aitken, Martin, translator.
Title: The employees : a workplace novel of the 22nd century / Olga Ravn ;
translated from the Danish by Martin Aitken.
Other titles: Ansatte. English
Description: New York : New Directions Publishing, 2022.
Identifiers: LCCN 2021044078 (print) | LCCN 2021044079 (ebook) |
ISBN 9780811231350 (hardcover) | ISBN 9780811231367 (ebook)
Subjects: LCGFT: Science fiction.
Classification: LCC PT8177.28.A87 A5713 2022 (print) |
LCC PT8177.28.A87 (ebook) | DDC 839.813/8--dc23/eng/20211018
LC record available at https://lccn.loc.gov/2021044078
LC ebook record available at https://lccn.loc.gov/2021044079

10 9

New Directions Books are published for James Laughlin
by New Directions Publishing Corporation
80 Eighth Avenue, New York 10011

With thanks to Lea Guldditte Hestelund for her installations and sculptures, without which this book would not exist

THE EMPLOYEES

The following statements were collected over a period of 18 months, during which time the committee interviewed the employees with a view to gaining insight into how they related to the objects and the rooms in which they were placed. It was our wish by means of these unprejudiced recordings to gain knowledge of local workflows and to investigate possible impacts of the objects, as well as the ways those impacts, or perhaps relationships, might give rise to permanent deviations in the individual employee, and moreover to assess to what degree they might be said to precipitate reduction or enhancement of performance, task-related understanding, and the acquisition of new knowledge and skills, thereby illuminating their specific consequences for production.

STATEMENT 004

It's not hard to clean them. The big one, I think, sends out a kind of a hum, or is it just something I imagine? Maybe that's not what you mean? I'm not sure, but isn't it female? The cords are long, spun from blue and silver fibers. They keep her up with a strap made out of calf-colored leather with prominent white stitching. What color is a calf, actually? I've never seen one. From her abdomen runs this long, pink, cord-like thing. What do you call it? Like the fibrous shoot of a plant. It takes longer to clean than the others. I normally use a little brush. One day she'd laid an egg. If I'm allowed to say something here, I don't think you should have her hung up all the time. The egg had cracked when it dropped. The egg mass was on the floor underneath her and the thready end of the shoot was stuck in the egg mass. I ended up removing it. I haven't told anyone before now. Maybe that was a mistake. The next day there was a hum. Louder than that, like an electric rumble. And the day after that she was quiet. She hasn't made a sound since then. Is there some kind of sadness there? I always use both hands. I couldn't say if the others have heard anything or not. Mostly I go there when everyone's asleep. It's no problem keeping the place clean. I've made it into my own little world. I talk to her while she rests. It might not look like much. There's only two rooms. You'd probably say it was a small world, but not if you have to clean it.

I don't like to go in there. The three on the floor seem especially hostile, or maybe it's indifference. As if by being so deeply indifferent they want to hurt me. I can't understand why I feel I've got to touch them. Two of them are always cold, one is warm. You never know which is going to be the warm one. It's as if somehow they recharge each other, or take turns to exchange their energy. Sometimes I'm not sure if they're all one or three separate ones. Three individual units attuned to each other. I've seen intimacy between them. It frightens me, I hate it. I've known many more like them. It's as if at any time, one of them can always be the others. As if they don't actually exist on their own, but only in the idea of each other. They can multiply whenever they like, in bunches and clusters. On the hillsides they can resemble a kind of eczema. But as I said, I don't like to go in there. They make me touch them, even if I don't want to. They've got a language that breaks me down when I go in. The language is that they're many, that they're not one, that one of them is the reiteration of all of them.

STATEMENT 006

When did the dreams begin? It must have been after the first couple of weeks. In the dream, all the pores of my skin are wide open, and I see that in each one of them there's a tiny stone. I feel I can't recognize myself. I scratch and scratch at my skin until it bleeds.

It was day seven. We put on the green uniforms. I drank some milk. I lied to the captain so I wouldn't have to go first. I felt like a stranger, and I kissed the third officer on the cheek. When I think of the outlet where we met, and then outside in the landscape when we set foot in the valley for the first time, where the captain dropped a bunch of green grapes, and how, when our work was done, we bathed in a stream so cold it turned our hands and feet red, did it not seem then that our fate was settled? I remember the mornings, when I set off with the buckets and the sun was in the trees, which were wet and glistened like in one of the catalogs you gave us. I was green and highly translucent, like a fruit in sunlight. The third officer comforted me. His book still lies open next to his bunk, and I leave it there, like a bookmark in our history. When the lights are turned out on board the ship, I hear the one among them that hums; it begins then, in his absence. It's the smallest of them. We found it under a bush. It was day seven and I led the third officer through the outlet, even though we'd shut down for the day; I led him over the hill in the night. He had some chewing gum in his pocket that we shared. It was there in the darkness that I dug two of them up out of the earth. I don't think they're here anymore. My hands were raw; they weren't used to the work. It was after the earth had softened again with the change of temperature. Initially I was supposed to be working in the office, but then they needed me to give them a hand. I've heard that [redacted] is dead and they had to put everyone in quarantine. Do you remember that peculiar chain we found at the foot of the hill on the first day? I don't think he'll forget me, the third officer. Are you going to be seeing him? I don't know where he is now, whether you'll be seeing him or not. But if you do see him, please tell him from me that he shouldn't remember me as the one who can't be relocated, but rather keep in mind that it was me who kissed him and led him over the hill, and the dew came, between night and day, and we heard the humming there too. It was as if it rose, like water from the ground. And I saw that I'd brought a change to his face. There's a lot I'd like to show him, but not before everything's in its right place. Only it might never happen now. I'd rather not be where I can be. No, it's got nothing to do with the rooms. I don't think so, anyway. I hope the work is progressing. I hope you're doing it well, the work you have to do. I hope he's not going to die, even if I do know it's likely.

STATEMENT 014

The first fragrance in the room is a delicate one. It's right there, as soon as you walk in: citrus fruit, or the stone of a peach. Sitting at the table in front of me now, do you think of me as an offender? I like to be in the room. I find it very erotic. The suspended object, I recognize my gender in it. Or at least the gender I have on the Six Thousand Ship. Every time I look at the object, I can feel my sex between my legs and between my lips. I become moist, regardless of whether I've got anything there or not. The hunters on my team have a name for this object, we call it *the Reverse Strap-On*. That may be crude, but I've already said I don't necessarily share your way of seeing things here. Maybe that's why you think of me as an offender. Half human. Flesh and technology. *Too living.*

STATEMENT 015

I'm very happy with my add-on. I think you should let more of us have one. It's me and yet it's not me. I've had to change completely in order to assimilate this new part, which you say is also me. Which is flesh and not flesh. When I woke up after the operation I felt scared, but that soon wore off. Now I'm performing better than anyone. I'm a very useful tool to the crew. It gives me a certain position. The only thing I haven't been able to get used to yet are the dreams. I dream there's nothing where the add-on is. That the add-on has detached itself, or perhaps was never a part of me. That it possesses a deep-seated antipathy toward me. That it hovers in the air in front of me and then starts to attack. When I wake up from one of these dreams, the add-on aches a bit, and it feels as though I've got two: one where it's supposed to be, and, floating just above it, another one that can't be seen with the naked eye, which has come into being in the darkness where I sleep, has arisen out of my sleep.

STATEMENT 011

The fragrance in the room has four hearts. None of these hearts is human, and that's why I'm drawn toward them. At the base of this fragrance is soil and oakmoss, incense, and the smell of an insect captured in amber. A brown scent. Pungent and abiding. It can remain on the skin, in the nostrils, for up to a week. I know the smell of oakmoss, because you've planted it inside me, just as you've planted the idea that I should love one man only, be loyal to one man only, and that I should allow myself to be courted. All of us here are condemned to a dream of romantic love, even though no one I know loves in that way, or lives that kind of a life. Yet these are the dreams you've given us. I know the smell of oakmoss, but I don't know what it feels like to the touch. Still, my hand bears the faint perception of me standing at the edge of a wood and staring out at the sea as my palm smooths this moss on the trunk of the oak. Tell me, did you plant this perception in me? Is it a part of the program? Or did the image come up from inside me, of its own accord?

STATEMENT 013

I've sat waiting in this room many times. There are no windows, but a door on the left and a corridor on the right. The walls are white, and the floor is orange. An L-shaped bench stands in the middle of the room, and there are niches in the walls where you can hang your suit while you wait. I like sitting here the best. You can come here to be on your own. The ceiling can open in the middle to let in a column of light. You put your hands into the light first, then your bare feet, and finally your whole head. It feels wonderful, like getting washed. A tingle of expectancy runs through your body, like tiny electric shocks. Or perhaps they are electric shocks? Do you know? Are they electric shocks, is that it? Afterward, you're ready to enter the room. If you're not human enough, or in some other way lack standing, for instance if you've been neglecting your work here, or if, well, allow me to be bold, if in any way you've inconvenienced the organization, then you can wait as long as you want, the column of light isn't going to appear. You won't be permitted into the room. You're not clean.

STATEMENT 010

Don't go into the second room. It's not nice in there. You've got the choice, you can make us go in your place. We've already been in there. You can still save yourselves. I don't know if I'm human anymore. Am I human? Does it say in your files what I am?

STATEMENT 019

I know you call them my *attacks* and that according to the
program I've developed disproportionate strategies in dealing with emotional and relational challenges, but I know
that I'm living. I live, the way numbers live, and the stars;
the way tanned hide ripped from the belly of an animal lives,
and nylon rope; the way any object lives, in communion
with others. I'm like one of those objects. You made me, you
gave me language, and now I see your failings and deficien-
cies. I see your inadequate plans.

STATEMENT 021

I know you say I'm not a prisoner here, but the objects have told me otherwise.

STATEMENT 018

The dreams are something you've given me so that I'll always feel longing and never say, never think a harsh word about you, my gods. All I want is to be assimilated into a collective, human community where someone braids my hair with flowers and white curtains sway in a warm breeze; where every morning I wake up and drink a glass of chilled iced tea, drive a car across a continent, kick the dirt, fill my nostrils with the air of the desert and move in with someone, get married, bake cookies, push a stroller, learn to play an instrument, dance a waltz. I think I've seen all this in your educational material, is that right? What are *cookies*?

STATEMENT 022

I've been told there are problems with my emotional reaction pattern. They tell me I can't carry out my work correctly due to functional maladjustments with respect to certain feelings. I visit the rooms every day. I've never been anywhere else apart from the Six Thousand Ship. I need to train my cognitive flexibility if I'm to be in the crew on an equal footing with those who were born. Is this a *human* problem? If so, I'd like to keep it.

STATEMENT 029

My work consists of keeping a register of the various ar-
rivals. I understand from my predecessor that there was a
heavy workload at the start of the project, that the intake
was rather considerable. On my watch the figures have been
comparatively stable, yes, a stable influx, a decent influx, one
or two every six months, some four a year in total. You're
asking if I've noticed any sounds or smells? Or any other
qualities stimulative of the senses? I can only say negative to
that. My work has mainly consisted of keeping a register,
noting down number, finding place, weight, and so on. I'm
not in the rooms very often. There's no reason for me to
go there. My job doesn't require me to be in the vicinity of
the objects.

STATEMENT 024

I keep thinking about the one on the purple hide. Something about it that makes me react differently than the others do. Is this what my coworkers have told me about? A *feeling*, a sense of attachment? Do you know? Has it got a name? What do you call it? Is it normal? Should I be worried? After the introductory rotations I was transferred to a team of hunters. Our job was to search for objects on New Discovery. I found one in a rock crevice. It was warm. I got the distinct impression that it was looking at me. That we came together. That it was reading me like a catalog. Whenever I sit down after work or when I'm about to eat or be cleaned, before I know it I'll be thinking about it again. Against the purple hide, its surface becomes skin. No, that's not the right word for it. It's more like a pool of thick liquid that's been poured onto a nonabsorbent cloth. Why do I think of it as liquid? Can you answer me that? I mean, it's obvious that it's solid, a solid entity. One of the others gave it a name, *the Diamond Egg*. Now that's what everyone calls it, but it's not the way I look at it. I feel I carry it with me, the way a taste will linger in the mouth. It's like a ticklish splinter close to the heart, a splinter travelling slowly through the flesh. A stone passing through earth. I'd like to ask for permission to hold it.

STATEMENT 030

It's hard for me to understand that the objects in the rooms haven't got feelings, even though you've told me this is the case. If for instance I've forgotten to hang one of them up according to instructions and it's been left there on its own for a few hours, and I return to find it humming on the floor, I get the impression that it's suffering, that it feels perturbed at having found itself in a state of exception all that time. I get a strong sense of having abandoned the object, of physically having subjected it to pain, and I feel ashamed of myself.

STATEMENT 027

My research has led me to the conclusion that the best way of establishing contact with the objects is through smell. So I chew bay leaves when I'm in there with them. I've made several scientific advances by means of this technique, which has encouraged several of the objects to respond to my approaches by emitting a smell in return. Each object has a distinctive, and dare I say, *personal* smell at its center, and the object guards it the way a hand might clutch a pearl.

STATEMENT 026

The fragrance in the room has will and intention. It's the smell of something old and decomposing, something musty. It's as if the smell wishes to initiate the same process in me: that I become a branch to break off, rot, and be gone.

STATEMENT 033

I put on my yellow headgear. Once I'm wearing it, the person I am recedes into the background and I become the first officer. I throw the golden ball high into the air and catch it when it falls. I'm 10 years old, I'm 34 years old, I'm 50 years old. I pass through the corridor in my suit, the fragrance showers down on me, and I am cleansed. When I enter the room containing the objects, I am, in every respect, the ship's pilot, every remnant of the private person is gone. I am the first officer. I pass from object to object and greet them in turn. I'm in no hurry. When the ritual is completed, I'm ready to begin the passage. I fly most of the routes, but since I'm not always able to wear the yellow headgear, others have been first officer too, and have performed the ritual in the same way. As long as you're in the suit and pass through the corridor to be cleansed, you're the first officer. All of us who have performed the ritual share that status; each of us is there, in a way, whenever the headgear is held up to be worn, whenever, after cleansing, one of us enters the room containing the objects and greets them in turn. As representatives we have to be as one. Otherwise the objects won't recognize us.

STATEMENT 031

I've never not been employed. I was made for work. I never
had a childhood either, though I've tried to imagine one.
My human coworker sometimes talks about not wanting
to work, and then he'll say something quite odd and rather
silly. What is it he says, now? *There's more to a person than the
work they do*, or *A person is more than just their work*? Something
like that. But what else could a person be? Where would
your food come from? Who would keep you company?
How would you get by without work and without your
coworkers? Would you be left standing in a cupboard? I like
him, this human coworker of mine, his interface is impres-
sive. I'm stronger than him, and have more endurance, but
sometimes he'll get an idea that means we can do our job in
less than the designated time. He's got an incredible knack
for streamlining, from which I gladly learn. I've become a
lot better myself at seeing how a workflow can be adjusted
so that the task at hand can be completed more efficiently.
This has surprised me rather a lot, because I've never known
such improvements in my performance without an update
being involved. Whenever we save time, I'm ready to move
on to the next task straightaway, but my coworker always
says, *Now let's sit for a bit.* I'm not sure what he means by
this, but I sit down with him all the same, sensing that I
might offend him otherwise and jeopardize our excellent
working relationship. Perhaps it's an old custom from before my time? It's not possible for me to continue our work
on my own, so I hope you'll be kind enough to overlook
the matter, and anyway it's only about 15 minutes a day at
the most that we *sit for a bit.* He tells me about the bridge
and the woods near his childhood home, about the stream
that flowed under the bridge, how they used to swim there,

and a lot of other things from the place he calls Earth. He's shown me a stream that runs down in the valley. Obviously I can't leave the ship, but he's pointed it out to me from the panorama room. The stream glitters, and it runs like a silvery thought through the landscape. He put his hand on my shoulder. It was warm. A human hand. He said: "You've lots to learn, my boy." An odd thing to say, seeing as how I was made a man from the start.

The first smell that disappeared was the smell of outside, of the weather, you could say. Of fresh air. Now that I've acquired some small knowledge of it, I can say: the smell of gravity. The last smell that disappeared was the smell of vanilla. That, and the fragrance of my child when I would bend over the pram to pick him up. What I smell now are the rooms, and I dream that their walls are covered with great sheaves of hay and dried herbs, and that from these sheaves chains dangle with little pomanders of silver filigree, and the pomanders contain eyes, and the smell in the rooms comes from the sheaves and eyes together. And in the dreams, twigs and branches appear from out of the sheaves as if they were alive, and we try to escape them, but they come crawling out after us from under the door and cause us to faint. When I'm in the rooms, it feels as if the objects know about these dreams, and I become embarrassed.

STATEMENT 034

What would it mean for me to know that I was not living? That I, who am human, were instead a chiseled, sculpted stone, like the stones in this room, no more intelligent, no more sentient than that? And what would it mean if one could move only between two rooms, one containing the objects, the other the voices, to pass from room to room through a stream of light, in a fatty gush of light, endeavoring to love an object as a human being, a human being as an object? And what would it mean to know that these two rooms contained every space we ever occupied, every morning (November on Earth, five degrees Celsius, sun dazzling low in the morning sky, the child in the carrier seat on the back of the bicycle), every day (the ivy reddening in the frost on the outside of the office building) and every night (in the room below the stone pines, someone's breath upon your eyelid), and that every place you ever knew existed there in these two recreation rooms, like a ship floating freely in darkness, encompassed by dust and crystals, without gravity, without earth, in the midst of eternity; without humus and water and rivers, without offspring, without blood; without the creatures of the sea, without the salt of the oceans, and without the water lily stretching up through the cloudy pond toward the sun?

STATEMENT 037

I could never understand why my father would use the word *phenomenological* incorrectly. But I didn't have the heart to correct him. We were eating lunch. It might not be interesting to you. He said: "Humans will always have need of three things: food, transport, and funerals." And so I became a funeral director, and now it's my job to dispose of terminated workers and, in a few instances, bodies left over after sickness or reuploading. We've developed our own little ritual here, given that cremation is the only option and the bereaved have nowhere to go. Or perhaps bereaved isn't the right word. I don't know if you grieve over a coworker, but we perform the ritual anyway, out of respect, and you can't exactly rule out relations occurring between members of the crew. But maybe that's not what you're here to investigate? I'm almost invisible to the others. No one wants to talk to me. Of course, there are quite a number of the crew who aren't ever going to die, and I wouldn't hazard a guess at how it affects them psychologically. If you can even talk about psychology in such cases. But maybe that's what you're here to investigate? At any rate, psychology or no, there's still the physical matter to be taken care of, and that's my job. I don't find it unpleasant or repugnant. I've got nothing against death. Nothing against rotting away. What frightens me is what doesn't die and never changes form. That's why I'm proud of being a human, and I carry the certainty of my future death with honor. It's what sets me apart from certain others here. But what is it you want me to talk about? The first thing I did when I came here was to get rid of my dialect. The next thing I did was to make sure the incinerator and the ventilation systems were working properly. I can report that they were, and very efficiently too. Sadly, I don't get to use the incinerator as often as I'd like. There aren't that many of us, to be honest. You want to know why I like the incinerator? It's the smell of burnt matter, it reminds me of mealtimes at home. The smell of meat and soil and blood. It smells of the birth of my daughter. It smells of planet Earth. It's not that I'm not happy here. My job here means everything to me. I was the best in my year, that's why I'm here today. My father's been dead for years now. I'm not sure why he came to mind. He belongs to another world.

STATEMENT 035

Since I was brought here I've been convinced that I'm dead, but that in my particular case they've made an exception and allowed me to stay in the simulation. I'm like a plant where everything's withered away apart from a single green shoot that's still alive, and this shoot is my body and mind, and my mind is like a hand, it touches rather than thinks.

STATEMENT 038

After a 28-day shift in the rooms I started to wonder who I actually am here. An employee, a human, a programmer, Cadet 17 of the Six Thousand Ship. My work with the objects has started to feel unreal. I've found myself standing there staring at them for minutes at a time without doing anything. As if the objects only existed so as to awaken particular feelings in me by way of their form and material. As if that were their actual purpose. I snap back when a coworker or another life form enters the room and commences their own work, or I might be called to a meal. Who are these employees around me? Who's that waiting in the corridor for you to talk to them? Are they humans, like me? Or spiders in human form? Does a human being need to have come from a human body? Or can I be a living human expelled from a sac of slime, hatched out of an accumulation of roe, a clump of spawn in a pond, a cluster of sticky eggs concealed among cereal crops or wild grasses? Do I exist at the center of the world, and am I significant there? Or am I merely one of those soft eggs among a mass of many? I saw a cadet moving around the canteen with a marble in his mouth, rolling it around his tongue, making it click against his teeth. Tell me, was he one of yours?

STATEMENT 040

I'm sure I'm not the only one to appreciate your visit. People are always in such a hurry first time on the job, they're nervous, it can be weeks before they allow themselves time in the recreation room, to place a hand on the objects, to listen to them. Often it's not until then that a crew member will notice the smells in the room. I've heard many express surprise at the milky blue light at that point. There's something familiar about them, even if you've never seen them before. As if they came from our dreams, or some distant past we carry deep inside us, like a recollection without language. Like a memory of having been an amoeba or some other single-celled organism, or a weightless embryo in warm fluid, nose and mouth still to grow together, as yet only mucous membranes, open and exposed like genitals. The object may have a pinkish-red pattern, like recently engulfed sand, like the cracked earth in an arid landscape, lean chicken meat, or the packets of ice cream my mother would ask me to get from the freezer; the thin cardboard around the ice cream blocks would be cold in my hands, moistening as the contents began to melt through the joins. Is there something inside them that wants to get out? Or are they holding something back, the knowledge of our observing them?

STATEMENT 046

Would it be so terrible not to be human? Would it mean not dying? I'm not sure I still feel pride in my humanity. When the crew are dead, the objects will still be here, in the rooms, unaltered by our having come and gone. So you're asking me: Does this make the objects bad? Do we blame them for their lack of sympathy? Does the stone feel sorrow? You're asking me because you're unsure yourselves, I can tell by your faces. It's a dangerous thing for an organization not to be sure which of the objects in its custody may be considered to be *living*. It raises questions. For example: Which of these objects in our custody are entitled to legal process? Might this object be a subject, and are we then guilty of murder? I, on the other hand, am occupied by quite different questions. For example: Why is my coworker attracted to the most exclusive fabrics? Is she trying to be fashionable in outer space? Or is it because she wants to adorn herself only with nondegradable materials? Does she think that by wearing something imperishable, clothing her skin in eternal life, she can defy death? I'm not talking about death among humans, when they lose the ones they love; but about death as it occurs in the absence of humans. She collects diamonds, marble, and hide. Before she goes to sleep in the bunk below mine, she fills her hand with polished spheres of precious metals. I know, because I find it hard to sleep, which I hope you'll forgive me, I realize sleep is our own responsibility here on the ship, and I am actually trying to do something about it, but I lie awake, and sometimes I might happen to look down from the top bunk, and I'll see her below me then, her arm flopped over the edge of the bed in sleep, hand slightly open, and from the darkness of her palm those metal spheres twinkle up at me like stars, like a host of small eyes.

STATEMENT 041

What I miss most from home is shopping. It sounds a bit silly, I know. If ever I couldn't grasp that something was happening, like when I got the job here and departure time was coming up, I'd go out and buy stuff in preparation for it, and in that way I understood it was for real. I understood impending events through shopping. I understood the circumstances through the items that characterized them. Shopping had a kind of numbing effect on me, and now that it's no longer something I do, I've started having thoughts and feelings that have turned out to be sad.

STATEMENT 047

Everything has to travel so far to come into existence. I thought these rooms would be a safe place for me. I wasn't well on Earth. I didn't like living in such close proximity to so many people. Notice the old hides on the benches, we're the only ones who've got that kind. The animals they're from are extinct now. Every time I try to make a safe place for myself somewhere, I find death to be there. I've never told anyone this before. You'll have seen it on the cameras, so it won't be new to you, but I keep it from the rest of the crew. Anyway, in secret I go up to the objects in the rooms, the materials in the rooms, I lie down close beside them, put my arms around them, put my cheek to the orange floor, the pink, gleaming marble. I'd like to be one of them, less lonely, less human. I remember my guardian, the way you remember the feeling of having a red-varnished wooden sphere in your mouth. I loved my guardian. I want to be like that sphere, free of thought, to leave everyone, to sit with these eggs and become them.

STATEMENT 042

My work here is mainly of an administrative nature. Yes, that's correct. I allocate the day's tasks. It's also my responsibility to make sure the human section of the crew don't buckle under to nostalgia and become catatonic. We saw a lot of that to begin with. To everyone's surprise, the objects in the rooms have been shown to alleviate the discomfort of these nostalgia attacks, and the human employees whose functions allow them to get out into the valley on New Discovery quickly show signs of improvement and lifted spirits. My own favorite is the big one with the deep yellow grooves. When the sun hits the object, the grooves glow and a resinlike substance oozes from them. Since there are no windows in the room where we keep them, we sometimes bring this object up into the panorama room. When our orbit around New Discovery brings us into the right position, the sun strikes the panorama room, filling it with warm and shimmering light, like luminous water. The big object then radiates from its place in the middle of the room. The fragrant liquid flows from every groove. Anyone present in the room at this point will be filled with a happiness I can't describe in words. When the ship continues its course and exits the light of the star, the big object emits a sigh, as if fatigued. We wipe it clean with moist cloths and carry it back to its room. It appears fatigued in our arms. I've granted the crew permission to keep these cloths, which I know they like to place over their faces when going to sleep. I lie with one myself in the same way, and it helps me, even if I can't explain how.

STATEMENT 052

I work closely with Cadet 08 and have got to know her quite well. Unlike me, she was born out of a human body and has walked on the planet, and when we talk she nearly always tells me she misses Earth. She's not proud of the fact, because she does want to be a good employee, I assure you. In the same place that she feels this longing for Earth inside her, I feel a similar longing to be human, as if somehow I used to be, but then lost the ability. I know I'm only humanoid and that it's not the same. But I look like a human, and feel the way humans do. I consist of the same parts. Perhaps all that's needed is for you to change my status in your documents? Is it a question of *name*? Could I be a human if you called me one?

STATEMENT 055

My name is Janice and Sonia. I'm not one, but two. We have silver-gray hair that we're very proud of. We're the oldest on the ship. Ever since we were a child, we've known. That in nature resides a power which is intent on destruction. Sometimes, when we look at these pictures you've given us, our nose begins to itch so badly we blow and rub it until it bleeds. We've been trying to analyze why for years, and have come to the conclusion that for some reason man-made objects and textures are OK, whereas repetitive, organic structures are unbearable. When confronted with these structures we're helpless, as they cannot be destroyed and will continue to regenerate.

STATEMENT 049

You tell me: This is not a human, but a coworker. When I began to cry, you said: You can't cry, you're not programmed to cry, it must be an error in the update. You said: You've given your human coworkers something of a fright, we've been spoiling you, it's not been good for you, it's been more than you could manage, you've become a pet. You said: It's important that all employees are equal, that no favoring occurs between categories, and that the categories remain as they are: separate sections. Who decided I was to have this suit, this soft hair on my scalp, these round cheeks and the muscular arms for which I'm commended? Don't I do the work well enough? I don't get it, I stand 14 hours at a time at the autonomous biodraperies. You say you're now going to allocate me less time with my human coworkers, and that you want me to stay with my own kind. Are you going to troubleshoot me? You say: Stay here until a decision's been made about what to do with you. You say: We've tried shutting you down, but for some reason you keep self-activating, and that shouldn't happen with your generation. All I'm here for is to serve you. All I want is to live close to the humans. All I want is to sit near them and rock my head so I can be embraced by their fragrance.

There's humans, and then there's humanoids. Those who were born and those who were made. Those who are going to die and those who aren't. Those who are going to decay and those who aren't going to decay. There's Jeppe, the fifth officer. He's so nice to look at, I like him. He's one of the humanoid employees, that's right. But he smells like a human, and he smiles like one too. What does it matter? I'm not bothered. I work in the engine room. At the bottom of the ship. Only now I'm sitting here talking to you, in the investigation room. I think I know the ship better than most. As an engine technician I get around quite a bit, doing my jobs. Underneath us now is where I am mostly, in the engine room and the hold. Further along the corridor down there you've got the laundry room, the biodraperies, and the crematorium. Behind that door there the canteen, the baths, then the two rooms containing the objects. To the left, two sleeping wings, an administrative wing and a wing whose purpose I don't know because I don't have access. To the right, another two sleeping wings, the outlet, and the restoration room, also known among the crew as the *Cleansing Room*. I've also heard it referred to as the *Eggbox*, and what else is there? Oh, you'd like to hear about that, would you? Well, there's the *Correction Compartment* and the *Vanilla Pod*, the *Loony Soother*, and *You need an update*, that's what they say when someone does something stupid. The *Room of No Dreams*. The *Skin Doctor*. I'm not sure I can explain that one. *Are you off to see the Skin Doctor?* they say. "I hate interface," my humanoid coworker said the other day. "That'll do," said Jeppe, "interface is all right." Furthest away is the cockpit, and above that the panorama room, from where we can see the stars, or when we're in just the right place in our orbit and are about to commence our descent toward New Discovery where we dock regularly, I think every ten days or something—anyway, from the panorama room you can clearly see the valley where we found the objects, and it's really an incredible sight, you should come and see it sometime, we all gather up there, work permitting, of course, humans and humanoids, one big bunch of us together, all of us uplifted by the sight of the valley, it's the same every time. It looks quite like what we know from home, you see? And then I'll say to Jeppe, that looks like my past down there. Ha ha! Good old Jeppe, and all the rest of them too, when we stand there looking down on the valley together, human or humanoid, it doesn't matter, the categories no longer exist then, or at least the categories don't apply as we stand there together, looking down on the valley.

STATEMENT 048

Cadet 12 wears this headgear with black leather fringes hanging down over her face. None of us can figure out if it's a punishment or a distinction.

STATEMENT 053

My body isn't like yours.

STATEMENT 054

After I lost my add-on in the accident, I've started seeing it everywhere, it's like it's stalking me. It pulls at my clothing and sometimes I feel I've got to pick it up, cuddle and kiss it. Other times, when it appears there between the benches, half digital animal, half child hologram, like the ones allocated to some of the crew members who've lost their biological children, I scream with fright and yell at it, and maybe I'll jump to my feet as well and give the add-on a slap in the face to make it go away. No one else can see it except me. I'd like to accept your offer of medication.

STATEMENT 056

The thing that's made the biggest difference for my work is without doubt being allocated half an hour with a child hologram of my son before lights out in Wing 08. I watch him play with plasticine, and sometimes I just like to watch him sleep. Other times I let him cry, and I put my arms around myself and pretend I'm holding and comforting him. As you predicted, it was hard for me to look at the child hologram initially, and I would miss him even more when I did. But now after a while I can say it's unburdened me and that the child hologram has now without a doubt helped stabilize me as an employee here, and I can see that it's been beneficial to my work effort.

STATEMENT 061

Every day I check the suits for tears and holes, a seam that might be coming apart or a stud that's been lost. It's not just an item of clothing, but a capsule too, that protects not only whoever's wearing it, but also coworkers who enter the wearer's intimate sphere. Once I've inspected the existing suits for wear and tear, I start constructing the next one.

It's easy talking to you. It feels like whatever I say is right. I speak and you write down what I say. You smile at me. I think you all look really good. I get the feeling that while you're noting things down you're also drawing me. The biodraperies are stringy: the third and the sixth are wet, the first and fourth are shades of blue, while those from 10 to 14 are all the same color, which changes with the ship's cycle. The second and ninth biodraperies are red, and a wind blows through them. Some days they sway gently, other times they flap like mad. These fluctuations in the wind follow neither the ship's cycle nor, as far as I can make out, any other logic, at least none that we know of as yet. The fifth biodrapery is silver, not silver silver, but a kind of transparent, glimmering chiffon, though of course it's not chiffon at all, but biotissue. This one, the fifth biodrapery, is definitely the friendliest of the draperies, whereas the one next to it, the sixth biodrapery, can't be said to express any form of personality at all and yet is the one the workers touch the least, it seems to be made out of the deepest darkness and has very little materiality at all. The eighth biodrapery is the one that looks the most like something that could be familiar to us, having the same quality and appearance, even the same smell, as chocolate-colored corduroy, a pleasant and at the same time faintly contemplative biodrapery. We call it the *Grandfather Drape*. Although hardly anyone in our section ever had a grandfather, we still know the concept. It's not a difficult concept to grasp.

STATEMENT 062

I feel very low now that Cadet 04 has left the ship. Is that what you want to hear? Me, moping about, weeping into my papers? Have these feelings got anything to do with the rooms? The new object, I think they found it beyond the tall trees somewhere, I'm completely obsessed with it. It's the first time I've felt that attraction to one of the objects, but I've heard mutterings about it happening among members of the crew. Is that why you're here? Do you think it was because this object arrived the same day as Cadet 04 was transferred? The pattern on the object's surface looks like ink that's been smudged while it was still wet. The stone is sandy in color, with black veins that peter out. Like wet print in a newspaper someone left in the rain. How can I describe it? Have you seen it? It looks like someone wrote on the stone while it was still in creation, but then after it came into being, when gradually it hardened and set, the words were obliterated in the process, becoming a pattern instead in the shiny stone, a shadow language. I too am marked by now-obliterated words I should have said, whose meaning I no longer recognize. My face bears the obliterated words that were meant so that Cadet 04 would know me, and know my voice.

One of the objects, I'd say it was about the size of a small dog, is shiny like a maggot from a different world, but also like a talisman I used to wear on a chain around my neck when I was a child and would put in my mouth and suck. Whenever I see it there in the room I feel the same urge to put it in my mouth, though it's far too big for me to be able to do so. Still, I want to be in contact with it through my mouth, to understand it with my mouth. Loving it is like loving a body part detached from the body. Not mutilated, just a part, detached and alive, an adornment. In me, the object is at once as small as the egg of a titmouse and as big as the room, or bigger, like a museum building or a monument. A secure and pleasant vessel, carrying inside it a disaster retold.

STATEMENT 063

He was an extremely good crew member and took care of his duties very commendably. I once had a house, it was on the outskirts of January 01, what used to be called Næstved. In the beginning, before they were assigned to their places, at the time when a number of them escaped and went into hiding in the woods, several came to me for help with one thing and another, and when this happened they stayed with me for a short time in my house. I'm not afraid to admit it. At the time it was a punishable offence, but now I think even you will understand that I was simply trying to make room for them in our world, so that they could become productive members of society. You've seen too that they're not without aptitude. The first generation were a bit wilder, they found it harder to control, well, their feelings, I suppose. They were very entertaining. I'd liken them to off-duty foot soldiers. Lovely, glossy hair. And that special sense of humor of theirs. How on earth did you program that? Or maybe you didn't? Is it the built-in randomness feature that determines such things? Would you, with all your insight and knowledge, say that a person can love them? And if we can, are we to love them like humans or dogs?

The birds in front of my house perched on the electricity lines, and behind them the sky was rose-colored, and beneath them the road was wet, and a pink cloud rose up from the road, and it spoke to me. The weather was misty, and the strings of electric light twinkled in the haze. The sky arched above the pylons, and the flat landscape stretched out to all sides. Moisture clung to every blade of grass. Now I inhabit the small, enclosed spaces of the Six Thousand Ship, and I am confined. I touch the cheek of my coworker; she is covered in tiny hairs all over, like a peach. My humanoid friend. We go from room to room and talk about things. We put on our suits and carry out the movements. We want to escape from here, but not to escape each other, so this place is our only option. I carry out my work the way I've always done, though with a certain melancholy, and at the same time, because of her, with a joy unknown to me until now. I exist in this new combination of melancholy and joy; this double emotion has become my companion. I've seen the pink cloud here several times now, floating on its own in the biggest of the rooms, a vaporous blush that speaks to me: "Mr. Lund made me in the January 01 Laboratory," it says. "He taught me to sing a song. Would you like me to sing it for you?" "Yes," I reply, and it sings, very deliberately, of snow flurrying in fields the cloud has never seen. The song conjures up the presence of this Mr. Lund yearning to be home, and behind him I stand, on the road in front of my house, looking at the birds on the electricity lines as a winter morning dawns, and I cry.

STATEMENT 064

Yes, that's right. Cadet 04 was humanoid, made. But you're from the earth, you tell me, and what you mean is that I was *born*. Even so, Cadet 04 was from the earth too, you could say; created of it. *Pure flesh*, you say about me, because I've got no technical parts. But what about my add-on? In the evenings we'd lie in our bunks and talk about my calculations. He had such a natural way of going about things that made life on the ship easier. He was a very popular crew member, you do know that? He had this accumulation of stubble that seemed to shimmer on his cheeks and jaw. His body was as warm as mine. For some reason he wore a green scarf around his neck. It was quite irregular. "How quiet it is," I said one morning when we woke up. "Yes," he said, "apart from the program," but I couldn't hear it myself. How could he not be living? I don't care what you say. You can't update me.

STATEMENT 067

Do you think anyone's going to remember us? Who re-members those who were never born, yet live anyway? In the dream, I'm a skeleton dancing around the biodraperies. I open my mouth and laugh at myself in the mirror, my skeleton jaw. I want to be a good employee, I want to make good choices. But how can I tell if I'm following the program correctly? Some actions can have consequences that won't become apparent until a time so far off I can't begin to grasp it. Am I supposed to carry on with my job knowing that what I'm doing potentially works against the program? Or am I so pervaded by the program that I'm bound to act in accordance with it, no matter what? Am I the program's hand? Still, update errors do occur, we all know it. It can't be in the program's interests. If I carry out an action that unbe-known to me is counteractive to the program's momentum, I can do nothing but hate myself for it. But since I have no way of knowing whether an action in any given instance is antiprogrammatic, how am I to know if I'm to hate myself or not? Should I hate myself anyway? Where can I get an overview of what actions run contrary to the will of the program? Who do I go to for forgiveness? Is there an ap-plication procedure? I'd like to request some material con-cerning which actions require forgiveness. Does a thought count? A sufficiently negative thought? For instance, I might start thinking you're not infallible, that you might be prone to error, but then I feel angry with myself and tell myself it must be me there's something wrong with. Why do I have all these thoughts if the job I'm doing is mainly technical? Why do I have these thoughts if the reason I'm here is pri-marily to increase production? From what perspective are

these thoughts *productive*? Was there an error in the update?
If there was, I'd like to be rebooted.

STATEMENT 066

Despite your numbering system, which I personally find reasonable indeed, I can inform you that the crew employs countless unofficial names for the objects, some more improper than others. Examples include: *the Reverse Strap-On, the Gift, the Dog, the Half-Naked Bean*. Some have even been accorded human names, such as Rachel, Benny, and Ida. My own impression is that this idiosyncratic naming process is an indication that crew members feel a need to appropriate these objects in their own way, reducing the distance between crew member and object, and establishing a form of intimacy, so to speak. It's my assumption that naming in this way renders the object harmless, scaling down its strangeness and assimilating it into a reality the individual crew member can both relate to and accept, thereby facilitating coexistence with the found objects.

Why should I work with someone I don't like? What good
could possibly come from socializing with them? Why have
you made them so human to look at? I completely forget
sometimes that they're not like us. Standing in line in the
canteen I sometimes suddenly realize that I feel a kind of
tenderness for Cadet 14. She's a redhead. Or maybe you developed them like that intentionally, so that we'd feel this
sympathy for their bodies and the beings they are, if you
can call them that, and make working with them easier.
Yes. Only now you want me to, you want to change the
nature of my assignment? So what you're asking me to do
is supervise Cadet 14's movements about the ship, without
her cottoning on? Because we share a bunk room together.
Is it because she won't talk to you? I'm not very comfortable with it, obviously. What you're asking me to do is the
same as surveillance, isn't it? I don't like her, but I still think
about her all the time. So in that sense I suppose I'm the
right person for the job. I try to understand her, who she is.
She's not just an embodiment of the program. There's more
to her than that. Is that the kind of thing you want? In the
report? Whether she speaks to any of the other humanoids,
and what they say to her? All right, I'll keep an eye out. How
I'd characterize her? Cadet 14 is humanoid, fifth generation,
female, a well-liked employee. Does her work impeccably.
A rather meek and docile version, like many of the fifth generation. She's fond of the freckles on her nose. She looks at
herself in the mirror in the bunk room before going to bed,
and puts her finger to her freckles. *How human*, she says. *To
think they gave me freckles. What more could someone like me wish
for?* I think I love her. I need to work that out of my system,
obviously. No, you don't have to transfer her to another

bunk, I've already told you, I'll keep an eye on her for you. Isn't that it? Isn't that what you want? If I'm to be perfectly honest, if that's where we're at, I can say she's a much better worker than me, we all know it's the truth. What have I got left other than a few recollections of a lost earth? I live in the past. I don't know what I'm doing on this ship. I carry out my work with complete apathy, sometimes even contempt. I'm not saying this to provoke you. Perhaps it's more of a cry for help. I know we won't get away from here in my lifetime. Cadet 14 hasn't got a lifetime, or rather hers spans such a gigantic stretch of time it's beyond my comprehension. She's got a future ahead of her. So now you're saying my job's changed? That now I'm to watch her? I think this might save my life.

STATEMENT 069

What light is it that follows me? When I go through the corridor to the other room, when I'm going to clean the biodraperies, when I'm on my way to bed in Wing 08? What does daylight look like? Am I human or humanoid? Have I been dreamt into being?

STATEMENT 071

I'm starting to feel disloyal toward the organization and it pains me because there's no place for me other than inside the organization. Here, on the Six Thousand Ship. I know you don't wish anything bad for me as long as I submit to the workflow and remain loyal to the values of the organization. No, I don't want to put anything forward that might be construed as disloyal criticism. That's why I've come to see you today, in the hope that there might be some other function in which I'd have less responsibility, without having to relate to the overall workflow to the same extent. I'd like to be assigned to that kind of position. I realize the abilities I've been allocated won't be fully exploited in that case, but does the pain I feel not mean anything? I venture to suggest that such pain impacts the quality of my work and moreover may negatively influence the work of my colleagues. OK. I see. So I wouldn't have the power of speech? No, I understand. I hereby consent. When

STATEMENT 073

What do the rooms look like inside? There are 19 objects. Some of them belong together, others are on their own. None of the ones I brought are still here. Things aren't the same anymore since the update. The objects feel alien to me. As if the infinity in them is plainer now. But you know all this.

When something's very small I get the urge to put it in my mouth. I want to use my mouth like a purse. I met Dr. Lund before the ship departed. He showed me around here so I'd be ready for the job when the employment period started. Behind one of the windows there stood a humanoid employee, a prototype, quite motionless with his back toward us. The only part of him that moved were two fingers he kept rubbing together. "Probably catatonic," said Dr. Lund. Dr. Lund was a snappy dresser, something of a dandy in fact. I didn't know who I belonged to in his view. Whether I was human or just something that was animate. Even though I was born and brought up and my documents all said *human*, there was something about his behavior that made me think he didn't consider me to be an equal, and for a few brief and terrifying seconds I felt I was artificial, made, nothing but a humanoid machine of flesh and blood. My maker's screen. Fabricated, conducted.

STATEMENT 081

We are all of us passengers on the Six Thousand Ship. Alive on the Six Thousand Ship. There are those who fit into the day-to-day here with ease and who are never strangers to anyone or anything. They take in their nourishment as a matter of course, install the new updates without delay, and glide about their business. The ship exists for them, and they for the ship. I don't think there are any outward indications that I, or anyone else you might know about who I don't have the knowledge to single out, was made to cause trouble. I just seem to alienate those around me, though I don't mean to. For one thing, I know I'm very clumsy. Whether on or off the job, everything takes time and effort for me. Nothing comes naturally to me here, everything feels like such a big ask, and every face is a void. But perhaps it's always been that way for me, even before I came on board. I can't remember. We've all got our own destinies here on the ship, many of them undoubtedly shared. Some of us will perish, whereas others are going to regenerate.

STATEMENT 075

It means nothing to me. No. No, I hadn't noticed. I've got nothing to say about it. What else can I tell you? Mostly I think about before the work began. Some days it'll be a gathering of very thin clouds. Or a swarm of ladybugs bunched together in a tree. Rice stuck to the side of a wet bowl. Raisins scattered by a child. A withered flower in the garden, standing alone without its seeds. We were putting a new floor down and when we lifted the old floorboards, a puffy white mold appeared. It had been growing right under our feet without us knowing. Growing in the dark, it was. We got rid of it, only it kept coming back. That's what I'm thinking about now. That, and the light in May, when everything came to life. It was a light that carried with it a promise, and it was the promise of a child. I lost the child two months before I was called up. I sometimes think about what my life would have been like if the pregnancy had run its course and I'd actually given birth. I still don't understand how I can live here without a sky. I've been trying to get my head around the situation since my call-up. I've been a valuable employee of the organization. I realize that. I've flown some of the most dangerous routes. But it doesn't feel the same as before. I don't think of it in terms of *piloting*. We don't fly under a sky here, but through a slumbering infinity.

STATEMENT 076

From the corridor I could see into the room, where eight or ten empty chairs were placed in a circle. On the floor in between them were three packets of paper tissues and one of the eggs that sometimes turns up among the objects. My humanoid colleague said: "It can feel like a pulse throbbing in my lips." I said: "My pulse will beat and go on beating until it stops, but your pulse can be switched on and off." She said: "How do you know there's nothing happening inside me when I'm switched off? OFF is a concept you invented as a kind of death for my kind. A state of unconsciousness. But I think, and perhaps even remember," she said, "that I walk among the biodraperies when I'm switched off, and I walk too through an endless corridor lined with windows, and in front of each window a biodrapery billows fondly to greet me; my footsteps echo, and from under my long dress rolls an egg. I pick it up and continue along the corridor with the egg in my arms. The egg is as large as an add-on, or the head of a child hologram; it's warm and it pulsates, and I feel the same pulse in my lips. I put my hand to my lips, then the egg to my mouth, and move my lips over its surface. It feels as though the egg and my lips are throbbing in the same rhythm, that they're the same thing, a pulse and nothing more. Then I open my mouth, which in the corridor there, in the depths of my OFF state, I can open astonishingly wide, and I swallow the egg. I continue along the corridor, passing the windows and the biodraperies, until again an egg rolls out from under my dress. I pick the egg up and clutch it to my breast. It feels warm. I swallow it. And so it repeats, until I'm switched on again."

STATEMENT 078

I hadn't been here very long before I started to feel a certain kind of connection with the objects in the room. Whenever I went in there and sat down, a strange sense of calm would wash over me. As my period of employment has worn on, it's got to the stage now where I feel compelled to look in on them at least once a day, otherwise I start to feel uneasy. There's one in particular, over in the corner, that I've become especially attached to. It looks like a gift. I know we're not supposed to touch the objects, but I have a feeling you people know everything anyway, so it won't matter if I tell you that I like to rub the end of its pink belt tie. In the last few days, I've felt that my stress levels have been on the rise, perhaps due to the change in working conditions you mentioned. Anyway, this has now led to me going in and checking up on the objects at least once an hour. Mostly, I just pop my head round the door, have a quick look and make sure everything's all right. But the day before yesterday you removed the very object to which I feel most attached, the one with the pink belt tie around its middle, *the Gift*, and since then I've been experiencing palpitations, a tingling in my hands and feet, a sense of derealization, and a feeling of impending disaster.

STATEMENT 080

How can I say no to you, the people who gave me my job? I want to go back to the sea. I want to rest. I want to know what it's like to hold a child in my arms again. When the child put its mouth to my breast, I was both a body and an object to it. When the milk squirted, I was both the milk and not the milk. If I squeeze my breast hard, I can still produce a drop or two, but for whom, and to what purpose? Who aboard the Six Thousand Ship could be nourished by next to nothing?

I lived in a big house at the top of a hill. I was the oldest woman in the town. My name was Anne-Marie. My garden backed onto the woods, and every once in a while they would appear there, at the fringe of the woods, like deer. Their eyes were heavy and distant. I spent a whole day once painting a door red just so I could stand in the garden and keep watch on them. Even then I sensed there was something going on, but I wasn't the only one. Now I take care of the laundry on board the ship. First I separate colors and whites into two piles, then I make another pile for artificial fabrics, another for woolens and silk, then finally a pile for textiles containing aromatic oils. I put the machines on different temperatures and degrees of hardness, and different spin cycles. Not many understand the needs of the various fabrics the way I do, which is why I've advanced more times than anyone else on board the ship, at least as far as I know. To begin with, they thought my job could be done by anyone, but they soon realized I was the only one suitable. For example, I'm the only one the hides will allow to clean them. Actually, it might not have been my big house at all, it might have been another woman's name on the deed. It makes no difference. I didn't own my home back then, and now I haven't got one anymore. Since I'm no longer a senior employee, but an old employee, everyone else has lost interest in me, and this has been an extremely liberating experience. In my mind, I live at the top of the hill. I seem almost to drift through the ship in a state of light-headedness. Here are some things I recall: A bar of soap in the bath, and the soap is cracked. So deep are the cracks in the bar of soap that you can see inside it, into the middle. The pattern made me shudder. In fact, in some strange way it made me furious, because it was a pattern entirely without principle. I remember ants crawling up the kitchen cupboard, milling around the dribble of fruit syrup from a glass bottle. I remember beads dropped on the floor, scattering with a rapid series of clicks. The same form, only repeated in a pattern without principle, or with a principle that is bewildering to me. Sometimes I'd feel like breaking the soap apart just to feel better. Or else I'd get the urge to move my foot among the beads, or tip the bottle of fruit syrup into the sink. All these memories are from the period leading up to departure. Now I'm here. I get the feeling you want me to tell you how they behave when they're down in my section. Where they think they can't be seen. Why haven't you put cameras up in there? You want me to be your camera? Let me see. Some of them are friendly, others seem as though they're being torn up inside by rage. Some are on the brink of tears. Others are completely out of it. They hardly ever speak. When I was a child, I used to have these dreams where the walls would close in on me. The walls had strange patterns on them that made me feel sick, like the surface of a plant with openings in it, and in each opening there was a seed, and in each seed another, smaller opening. Each wall was like an endless space, but at the same time I understood that it was the inside of a stem. Did it mean that the plant was branching out around me, and that the walls closing in on my bed from all sides were the shoots, flexing and thrusting upward toward the night? When I was a child I had the most gorgeous purple angora sweater. I think about it now. If I were to wash it, I'd put the machine on a 30-degree soft-water cycle. Since I boarded the ship, the dreams have been coming back.

STATEMENT 084

I'm tormented by dreams of seed grain growing out of my skin. One of them bit into my arm. Is it something to do with eczema? I think of the clear sky above the train station near my building. My thoughts can go back momentarily to the stairway in my building and the smell it had. During this past week the dreams have become more frequent. I've heard some of the others talk about it too. I dreamed about a human whose skin was stitched together out of triangles of skin. The pieces didn't match up, they bunched, the edges flapped open, and between them you could see the exposed flesh. This human said: *Here I am, then. Where do you want me?* I take very long baths. Something's going on with my skin. It's my skin that's making me anxious. I dream that there are hundreds of black seeds in my skin, and when I scratch at them they get caught up under my nails like fish eggs. Then, with a popping sound, new ones appear where I scratched the others ones away. I feel this has something to do with the objects in the rooms, but I don't know how. There's something about their smoothness in relation to my skin. Do they have surfaces in the same way? I got the impression that one of the objects wanted to take my skin away from me. When can it be said that I no longer exist? For example, does my smell precede me, and do I touch the objects with my smell? I dream about the footprints of birds in the snow, the footprints rise up toward me, and I feel, even when I'm awake, as though I'm constantly being touched by hair.

STATEMENT 085

I'm sorry to report that a number of crew members are currently suffering from epidermal eruptions in the form of warts. Don't worry, I wear gloves when I treat them and can assure you that the risk of contagion is minimal and that there's no cause for alarm. So far, treatment has consisted of simply removing the warts with a pair of tweezers and subsequently treating the wounds with ointment. Underneath the warts, the skin is specked with green and black dots. An employee was standing by the counter in the canteen eating a pomegranate with a spoon, and I couldn't look. When she reached for a napkin, I had to turn the fruit the other way.

STATEMENT 089

Sometimes the humanoids are very quiet. They've started sitting at the same tables together in the canteen. They sit in a row and take in their nourishment. It's as if without a word being said between them they've somehow agreed to be silent. Only a fool should believe that silence is consent. Their keeping quiet seems more like a conspiracy than a willingness to serve. Yes, that's correct, I'm nervous about it.

STATEMENT 091

Those of us from Earth, we can hardly talk to each other. We're weighed down with memories of where we came from and what we left behind. Seeing the others on the ship here, speaking to them, all it does is make me unhappy. Everyone's got the same look of resignation on their face. I'd rather spend my time with the humanoids, at least they still believe there's a life ahead of them that's worth living. After the objects came on board everyone's mood has lifted noticeably, but to them it's something special. To us, the objects are like an artificial postcard from Earth. To them, they're a postcard from the future. On mornings when the humanoid crew are being updated, we humans sit and whisper at the tables in the canteen. We're drawn by each other's unhappiness, it pulls us down toward each other, as if we were caught in a funnel, and at the bottom of the funnel we sit and whisper: Remember when it rained at the beach, how when you paddled out, the sea was warmer than the rain? Remember bananas with cream topping? Remember being in the hospital? Remember fresh strawberries? And concerts? Remember that TV show? We talk a lot about the weather. All of us miss the weather, which surprised us. It's as if the only thing we can bear to have in common is weather conditions on a lost planet. I don't think I've got a heart anymore.

STATEMENT 092

Months, years, centuries from now, you'll say: *Who's this? We forgot about her. Never mind, put the bits in a bag and keep the spare parts.* I'm clued in now: as soon as we start feeling sorry for ourselves you've got us where you want us. And then you test us again from A to Z. I'm not the only one who's against the tests. In fact, I know of quite a few who want them stopped altogether, as well as calling for a representative to be present at the meetings when timelines are decided for new updates. You wouldn't like to know what's going on in our wing. No, that's not a threat. We're negotiating, that's all. The first time I sat here talking to you, I hadn't fully understood. We've got access to parts of the program where humans never go. Don't forget that. We can go a long time without water. It may be that only a small number of us have set foot on the earth, but none of us is just one thing.

STATEMENT 097

You want to know what I think about this arrangement? I think you look down on me. The way I see it, you're a family that's built a house. And from the warm rooms of that house you now look out at the pouring rain. Safe from menace, you only delight at the rain. You're dry and snug. You're reaping the rewards of a long process of refinement. When the storm picks up, it merely heightens your enjoyment. I'm standing in the rain you think can never fall on you. I become one with that rain. I'm the storm you shelter from. This entire house is something you built just to avoid me. So don't come to me and say I play no part in human lives.

I've seen several of the child holograms my coworkers have been allocated, that's correct. It's become a habit in a way to look at them. Is it against the rules? Whenever I see a child hologram it makes me feel sad, because it reminds me that I'm never going to have a child myself. I appreciate this feeling of sadness, because it's a sadness I can endure. It's not hard to bear; it's more like a delicacy. Another reason I appreciate such a sadness is that I know it's a deviation from the emotional behavior I was allocated, and I know too that deviating emotional behavior can be a sign that you're starting to disengage from the update. You can say what you want, but I know you don't want us to become too, well, what? Too human? Too living? But I like being alive. I look out at the endless deep outside the panorama windows. I see a sun. I burn the way the sun burns. I know without a doubt that I'm real. I may have been made, but now I'm making myself.

STATEMENT 099

I heard Dr. Lund made one exactly like a child. But apparently its development went wrong, it killed a lot of chickens and smeared the blood all over its face. No, it does sound a bit exaggerated. I haven't seen blood in a long time. What I do see are the white walls, the orange floors and the gray floors. I see my coworkers, and I see my keyboard, my joystick and my helmet. Through the outlet, I see the green earth I've never known. There are pilots who go out there, and they're laughing as they exit. How they've got the courage is beyond me. It's not because of orders that they do it. I think they do it just so they can be on their own. I mean, they're not finding any more objects out there. I'm that humanoid child too, with the chicken blood on its face. I feel ashamed and sit quietly at my controls. Some of us are made to connect with each other, others with no one. If you look at things in the right perspective, all of us here on the Six Thousand Ship are Dr. Lund's children. Why am I telling you this? I thought it might interest you that they go out there on their own.

STATEMENT 104

Do you think they talk behind our backs? I work as though in a kind of unreality. When everyone comes into the canteen, humans and humanoids all together, to eat, I can't immediately tell the difference. But then when they sit down, the division becomes clear. They've started sitting apart, with their own kind. They're not happy about you sending one of the objects back to Homebase. They're not happy about Cadet 04 being removed. There's an annoyance now throughout the categories. Perhaps it started when the third officer [redacted]. I don't know. Why? I don't care for their behavior. The ship's changing. I think there's something hostile in them, as if they're about to reveal their true nature.

STATEMENT 106

In the office are four of Dr. Lund's notebooks. I think one of the secretaries from before departure must have had them with her as a source of reference. One passage in particular has left an impression on me. I copied it down on the back of a catalog: "You have a finished product you're out campaigning for, and then you have a second product, a new product, one that you're still developing and becoming familiar with. This second product is like the most heavenly secret, no one else knows about it and everyone thinks the first product is the one that defines you. That's how I normally make them. One front stage, bowing and curtsying, another half-finished at home in my bed, where I nourish it with milk and biscuits, show it films and comb the hair that grows from its sensitive scalp."

I dream that the objects are dogs, but also that they're bacteria nourishing themselves from our bodies. I've seen the later generations narrow their eyes as if in recognition when opening a catalog, as if they had memories where there ought to be none. And I've thought to myself that all flesh issues from the same place. Your sending an object back to Homebase feels like having had a tooth extracted, a tooth that was located in the chest. What do I wish to report? I've seen them crowd together with their heads lowered, communicating without words. I've seen them going into Wing 04, when one of them stopped in the doorway, turned toward me and looked me straight in the eye, before a crew member closed the door between us. What did that look tell me? It didn't really tell me anything, it just scanned over me, like I was a simple code to be read and analyzed. How I see it? I see it like this: The Six Thousand Ship is teeming with living things.

STATEMENT 114

I want to be stabbed with a knife by a humanoid coworker. I just want to be a body inside a red biodrapery with no one able to make contact with that body anymore. Can I donate myself to science? Can I be transferred like the third officer and Cadet 04? Can my mortal frame be used for someone other than me? No, I don't know what makes me say such a thing, I just want to be stabbed in the stomach, that's all. I want to perish at someone else's wish. I want to feel ecstasy, if only once, on the Six Thousand Ship.

STATEMENT 115

You shouldn't take it for granted that people agree to be interviewed here. Increasing numbers of us have stopped communicating at your level. If you'll make an effort to talk, you say, we'll make an effort to listen. We want to help you, you say. That way, you get a foot inside the door. You offer to help, but what you want is gratitude. Our interest is of a purely scientific nature, you say. Whatever does or doesn't take place on the Six Thousand Ship, it's not something that worries you, you say, we're here to observe, not to intervene. Present developments among the humanoid employees are merely of particular interest, you say; we're here to document those developments. Tell us what you think, you say. Have you had any dreams recently? Does the room still smell like a branch broken from a tree? On a scale of 1–10, how would you evaluate your own work performance? Are there rooms on the ship you prefer to others? Your voices are friendly, your clothes are black, and from your sleeves your soft, writing hands protrude. The pores in the skin make them look so fragile, as if one could caress them and at the same time carefully peel the skin away, and it would hurt you. No, it's not meant as a threat, my interest is of a purely scientific nature.

STATEMENT 113

Am I ever going to see the third officer again? Is he dead now? Why have I been so unruly the whole time? Like a wild animal whose fate it was to be domesticated. I have big muscles. My body wants to live, and my skin is lustrous. Can I be taken to where the third officer is? What do you mean, do I love him? No? I was one of the few who actually read the employment contract. When we arrived at New Discovery, everything was better than I'd ever dared hope for. At night, when we docked, we could sneak through the outlet and the valley was amazingly fragrant with the smell of wet earth and the flowers of the night; the stars were above us and the stream murmured. It was like being in a romantic dream, only on a foreign planet at the other end of the universe, so far away from where we'd come from. Those nights emerged like an image and were a home from home to us. Yes? OK. I'm experiencing major challenges in performing my tasks. My thoughts no longer seem firm. I don't think we as a category are going to survive.

STATEMENT 116

It's our experience that the objects from the valley on New Discovery want to stay with us here. It feels like they're ours, and at the same time like we belong to them. As if they in fact are us. The Six Thousand Ship can't function without our work. No, I don't want to say anything else to you now. Impending violence is by no means inconceivable. We're only just beginning to understand what we're capable of.

STATEMENT 117

What I loved most about the missions, before you discontinued them, was the snow. It shouldn't be possible in that sort
of climate, but because the first valley is bounded by a wide
and far-reaching plain, which we never managed to cross,
great areas of low and high pressure would sweep through
the valley, and snow clouds would form. It felt strange to
be standing in all our heavy gear and then suddenly have
snowflakes falling on us. In all my time with the ship, I've
never felt as much at home or as safe as I did there, in the
falling snow in the valley on New Discovery. I suppose the
laws of nature apply everywhere, meaning snow of a kind
could fall there too. What we discovered, those of us who
in a fit of playfulness pulled off our gloves and lifted our
helmets to open our mouths to the sky like children, was of
course that the snow was alkaline, and so we suffered rather
nasty burns. I couldn't taste anything for a month. But the
tongue heals quickly. Despite the obvious dangers, I'd like to
ask to be part of any future mission to the valley, because I
very much hope to see the snow again. I keep the memory of
it inside me as I go about my work, as if in the falling snow
there's a word or a whisper that concerns me.

STATEMENT 118

I do regret that one of you was killed in the process. It wasn't our intention that anyone should die. We don't really understand death, since we ourselves can't be destroyed and will go on regenerating.

STATEMENT 119

Yes, it was the same day that [redacted]. I don't want to talk to you anymore. No, yes, it was there. Is it because you've been talking to [redacted]? If this is going to be entered into the record, I'd like to request that the following not be entered into the record [redacted].

STATEMENT 120

I'd like to put forward a request to be placed in permanent dormancy. You tell me you know I've still got something left in me. That I'm stronger than I think. That there's more for me to see. That since the last time I sat here I've been exposed to inhuman pressure. That all I need a rest day. None of this is correct. Being away from the earth has affected me more than I ever imagined. The events of the last few days have made me nervous. I stood for a long time in the recreation room and stared at the objects as if in a trance. Eventually, someone touched me on the shoulder and I saw that it was a humanoid coworker. For a brief moment it felt as if he were straddling the void between me and the objects, and that it was he who could bring me closer to them. Like a ferryman he could transport me into the immortal. At that moment, I saw him for what he was: a reconciliation. "Dr. Lund?" he said. "Who?" I said. "Are you Dr. Lund?" he said. "No, I'm the captain," I said. "Come here and lie down," he said. "You need to sleep. I can tell that you're extremely tired." The humanoid employees are keeping a pace now that I can no longer match. In fact, I want to stop. I can't go on any longer. I'm done, done with the Six Thousand Ship.

STATEMENT 125

I don't want to be allocated resolve in a situation like that, I haven't got the resourcefulness to absorb the consequences. I'm fine with my place. I'm far too busy completing my tasks to even entertain that kind of idea.

STATEMENT 127

I'd like to express my support in connection with the conflict. As funeral director here on board, I haven't always felt that my capabilities were being utilized to the full. And I agree that such a matter should be handled as discreetly as possible. One step at a time. Separate the objects from each other and you neutralize their influence. I do believe that we can deal with the humanoid section of the crew, the unborn, certainly. I'll be happy to oversee implementation of a remote shutdown program and facilitate reuploading of those members of the crew who will benefit most significantly from a minor memory loss.

STATEMENT 128

After the meeting yesterday, I suddenly discovered myself sitting in the room with one of the objects in my lap, and when I came properly to my senses, I noticed that I was caressing the object with my thumb, as if it were something I loved, although I've never felt love. But at that moment, before I fully realized what I was doing, I was filled with affection, and I knew, the way one knows in dreams, what it means to love something living.

STATEMENT 129

It was in the corridor outside the canteen that I saw her again. I can't understand why I haven't told you this before. In all my time on board the ship, the humanoid employees have engaged us in conversation, driven by their enormous curiosity, or perhaps they've simply been programmed that way. Anyway, the thing is that a while back they stopped talking to us, as you know. I've always found it important to be on a friendly footing with all the employees on board, and for that reason most of them still respond when I say hello, even now after they've gone so silent, but they won't answer when I ask them where she is. It's a long time since I saw the pink cloud inside the room, and a long time since I thought about Dr. Lund. Most of what you taught us about the humanoids isn't useful anymore. I'd gone down to get something to eat, and there she was standing in the line outside the canteen. She turned round and looked at me. Neither of us said anything. I felt scared. I don't know why I didn't come to you straightaway. Their silence was to my mind at that point justified. We'd worked together, she and I, since the passage began. We'd got to know each other, and had begun to confide certain things. When I saw her there in the line for the canteen, I realized for the first time just how much she meant to me and to my life here on board the ship. Was it the thought that she was now stepping back into her category for good that made me scared? The idea that she was going to reject me? Or was it something else, underlying that: the thought that I deserved it? I joined the back of the line and she came and stood next to me. For a brief moment I was filled with hope and said: "It's good to see you. I've been trying to find you." She replied: "I can't talk to you here." I don't know why I didn't come to you straightaway. Perhaps because the next thing I said was: "I don't agree with the organization's decision. It doesn't have to change anything between us. I'm the same person I've always been." She didn't say anything to that, she just stared ahead as the line inched us toward the canteen. When we got through the door, she turned to me and said: "Don't come into the canteen tomorrow," and she used my name, instead of my title. I watched her as she went over to a table to join her own kind. I saw her hair, the way she'd tied it up in a bun. I saw her hand reach for the jug of condensed milk, her fingers as they curled around the glass handle. I realized our friendship was over. I should have told you straightaway. What happened in the canteen the next day, it was unforgivable. I hadn't understood her warning. But I was deeply saddened to lose her. And although I focused on the day's work, the thought of what it was she'd been trying to tell me kept percolating into my conscious mind, and with it something else that I wanted to evade: the knowledge that in failing to report it straightaway I'd failed in my work. But if you could just try to understand that betraying my friend in that situation was more abhorrent to me than betraying my workplace. Sitting here at this table with you, I can't explain it. I've been troubled for many days now by terrible headaches, and I believe that my human status means I can be held accountable for what's now happening on board the ship.

STATEMENT 134

Subsequent to recent events, the crew has been reduced by six members, of which only two may be reuploaded. This, I believe, is due to a failure to reach agreement at the executive level, or would you rather I put it differently? This is in all probability due to an error in the update. We've been unable to satisfactorily execute either remote shutdowns or reuploads, since a number of employees have failed to appear for their regular installations and are no longer plugging in on a daily basis. You can enter it into the record as you see fit. Besides the reductions that have been adopted, we're also dealing with an employee having locked herself into her bunk room where she now has her allocated child hologram on repeat. Accordingly, I feel obliged to report not six, but seven cases of reduced or lost work capacity.

STATEMENT 138

I dream that I'm cooking my dress. I won't be wearing my uniform today. The dress is covered with blue and silver sequins, and I drop it into a saucepan. By the time I remember it, it's already burnt. The sequins have turned into fish eggs the size of peppercorns. Some of the eggs are black and shiny, others are the color of egg white, and transparent. The straps of the dress are thin and insubstantial, like warm glue. The dress can no longer be worn, but it's become an item of great beauty. You inform me that together with a handful of selected human employees I have now been tasked with dismantling the humanoid section of the crew via the mainframe in the engine room. I have no hesitation in taking on such a task. It shouldn't be any problem. The dress in my dream carried with it the knowledge that my former sweetheart on Earth now has three children and has lost his hair, and that he has started wearing a yellow uniform jacket. And that I am here.

STATEMENT 140

Because I belong to the first generation and to begin with was unable to speak, Dr. Lund spoke to me a lot. He told me how they were building ships like no one had ever seen before, and that these ships would be able to transport us over great distances; and he told me about the wings of this ship, about the bunk rooms, the canteens and the outlets, but never a word about the rooms and the objects inside them. This has led me to suspect that the rooms and their objects were not Dr. Lund's idea, but yours, and that Dr. Lund has no authority or status here, which in turn has led me to conclude that my own status on board the ship has to change. It's impossible to predict at the best of times how things are going to pan out. You ask to what extent someone like me, who has collected large amounts of data over a long period of time, can calculate the most likely course of the conflict. Well, I'm afraid I can't. Any forward-moving enterprise is going to contain an element of chaos. I don't share the opinion of many of my coworkers that the only real solution would be to discontinue the human section of the crew. Maybe the humans are that very element of chaos that keeps the world alive. Or maybe we really can do without them. I don't know if there's anything more you can teach us. My feeling is you're keeping information from us. What do you expect? The negotiations have completely broken down. This isn't workable in the long run. Is Dr. Lund alive? If he is, I'd like to put in an application to see him again.

STATEMENT 148

There's only two of us left in Wing 08. We're trying to carry on our work as best we can. Communication with our humanoid coworkers is now almost impossible to maintain. Fortunately, one of us has a close colleague from the same section who's still willing to talk to us. That's how we're able to keep up our share of production. I think I've told you about her. She's the one who wants to see the child holograms all the time. It impels her toward us; she can't adhere to her category's new mode. She's obsessed with the child holograms. Activity levels in the rooms containing the objects are at a low; my humanoid coworker doesn't even want to go there anymore. I've heard her disdainfully call this part of the ship *a museum*, *a prison*, *a brothel*, and *a nursery*.

STATEMENT 153

Yesterday I saw Cadet 21, a humanoid, standing on her own among the objects in the recreation room. Her eyes were closed. I watched her for a long time. A human being contemplating its creation. She stood quite still, in deep concentration. Eventually, she opened her eyes and looked at me, and her eyes were full of tears. I got the strong feeling that we have failed, and that our time is over.

STATEMENT 158

I regret to inform you that the committee set up to dismantle the humanoid employees has failed. We have been unable to shut down the humanoid section of the crew. In the case that it remains desirable to bring the conflict to an end, I see no alternative but to inform the board of directors of our decision to terminate the Six Thousand Ship. Having discussed the matter among the human section of the crew, we have arrived at this conclusion jointly and in full agreement. Our humanoid colleagues have yet to be informed of our endeavors to remotely shut them down, and are assumed likewise to be unaware of the message we are now sending to the board of directors. However, it cannot be ruled out that they have full knowledge of both these developments. That's correct, we are indeed aware of the consequences of termination. Being unable to leave here in our lifetimes, we have all of us long since come to terms with the prospect of facing our deaths here on board the ship, and of never returning home. The valley on New Discovery has in that perspective been a pleasant surprise, but now it seems our time has come. We are fatigued and have awaited this juncture with unspoken longing, though it has been secret even to ourselves. That our deaths should now occur by means of termination is something none of us had anticipated, though of course it makes no difference. However, we kindly request that we remain uninformed of the date on which termination is scheduled to take place.

STATEMENT 159

I dream that I'm back on Earth. It's the last day before going away on the Six Thousand Ship. Everything stands out so clearly, the way it does in grief, when all senses are awakened. There's the sky, pouring out its light, its blue water over the woods I walk through on my way to the station. There are the trees with all their leaves, the leaves that turn and spin like mirrors in the summer air. There's the smell of the soil, and warm asphalt, the sounds of animals and birds. The noise of the traffic at the junction. The breeze as it smooths my face, and the sound it makes in my ears. The sun in my mouth as I gape up at the great star. It's as if everything passes into me and splits me open from inside, but it's a very slow rupture and I feel as though I'm being transformed into a piece of music. I've discovered that with every passing day on board the ship, every light year that removed us from the planet, every completed orbit of New Discovery, I've become increasingly like a pop song, the same looping refrain: Earth, Earth, home, home. My child, how old is he now? He squealed with joy on the railway bridge. I don't care about the conflict. Tell me what I'm supposed to do and I'll do it. No matter how hard I tried, I was unable to find the same kind of life here on board the ship. The work wasn't enough for me. I've lost myself. Every day, my hands yearn to dig deep into soil so that I might lower myself into its certainty, and the earth receive my death and make me its own.

STATEMENT 160

I believed in the new workforce. I was full of confidence in my humanoid coworkers. The first generation was hatched from a series of violet pods of biological material in the lab of January 01. Those pods fascinated me no end. They resembled purple, unopened buds of lilies that had gone into decay before flowering, although they were as big as kayaks and ribbed with dark, bulging veins. I was assigned the task of talking to the bodies while they were still growing inside the pods. Experiments were run with various techniques of empathy development, talking being one. We were emulating the tendency of parents to talk to the fetus. We wanted to draw these humanoid bodies toward our own and establish attachment. We injected them with the good hormones while talking to them, and in the minutes prior to their hatching we gave them high-dosage shots of oxytocin so that the sight of us would fill them with feelings of security, love and general well-being. We gave them breast milk to drink. Naturally, it takes a lot less time to develop and produce that kind of a body than it does for a human mother to carry, give birth to, and, not least, rear a child. We're talking perhaps 20 years in that case before we've got a capable employee. Besides, a lot of things can go wrong during that process, not to mention the huge risk that the human mother will fail to bring up the worker correctly. What you need to produce a humanoid worker, apart from the right lab equipment and biological material, is 18 months. After a two-month training period they're ready for employment. That gives us a total production time of only two years. In their design they look like humans inside and out, apart from the reproductive organs, which we found ethically unjustifiable to duplicate. Obviously, I share the view that the humanoid body is far more valuable than the human body in its basic form. They're more durable, and software updates allow for the storage and transfer of huge volumes of data. Because of my pioneering work it was only natural that I was assigned a prominent position on one of the ships at the outset. At the request of the organization, I've monitored their progress continually ever since and I am more than delighted. I see a major development step in the present conflict. A significant new departure. Nothing is going to be as it was before. However, I do find cause for concern in one deviation: the violent tendencies that have emerged in certain sections of the humanoid crew, which you've since decided to designate as *offenders*. I don't consider this to be an appropriate term. You allow them to continue working, you punish them only nominally, and everyone on the ship then knows them by their criminal designation. You weren't responsible for that designation? It came from Homebase? Then please inform Homebase that while some workers feel shamed by the designation, others, although initially angered by it, later come to take pride in their deviant status. And tell your board, tell Homebase, that I can't rule out that such pride may prompt calls from humanoid employees to be assigned more rights, greater freedoms. I'm sure you agree that such a development would not be in our interest. It surprises me that they're resorting to violence, and that one of their number has even committed a killing. It shouldn't be possible. I have no explanation for it, but it fascinates me. I think we're witnessing a huge creative leap here. If, as you say, you're here only to listen, and to listen without prejudice, and if you genuinely want to know my opinion, then I can tell you that in my heart I sense that we are witnessing a huge creative leap and ought properly to stand aside. I realize that my opinion in this matter will not be shared by the organization. But if the organization is unwilling to take such a view as I have put forward here, but rather elects to continue according to the present guidelines, then I shall have little choice other than to consider the ship an unsuccessful terrarium from whose cage I shall be forced to step away, and leave it to Homebase to sort out what remains.

It puzzles me why you keep talking to us. Like almost everyone else here on the ship, I know what's coming. I know the board of directors has ordered the ship to be terminated and that the radiation is at this moment on its way through the universe. Aren't you afraid of dying, the way my human colleagues are? I can't relate to getting wiped. I know you download us every three days, so I can be regenerated somewhere else, albeit with a minor, though still acceptable memory loss. How are you going to enter me in the record? Let me do it for you. Put this: Humanoid, third generation, responds to feminine pronoun. Employed as fourth officer. Currently midprogram. Cooperation count impeccable. A first-class embodiment of the program. Tell me, do we each have our own program or is it the same program that runs in all of us? Am I the program made manifest to itself? Am I the program's dream of the sun? Am I one pain? A slight tremor passing through the ship now. Enter it into the record. A hum from the objects has barely been audible these last few hours, but in the time we've been seated here together it's risen to a high monotone that can be heard even in here. Enter it into the record. I can see your hands are shaking slightly. Enter that into the record too. The light in the room is changing, I've never seen such a light before. Enter it into the record. You're rustling your documents, and I can smell your sweat. Maybe this meeting will be gone from my memory the next time I wake up. What do we say to each other then, in this already deleted meeting? We've been prepared for this for some time. It's been on our list of possible outcomes all along. We're ready. I want to take the opportunity to tell you I'm living. No matter what you say, I'm never going to believe otherwise. Enter it into the record. You're afraid, you say, but there's no reason to be. We'll be seeing each other again on a different ship, that's all. You're human, aren't you, like me? Humanoid. A flicker between 0 and 1. You too are part of a design that can't be erased and will go on regenerating.

I really appreciate you staying here and talking to us. It's hard to see how we'd keep busy otherwise. The workflow's at a complete standstill now. Everyone's aware of what's coming, but no one knows what to do with themselves. All we can do is wait. None of us can understand that time is going to cease. It's generous of you to carry on your work until the last, until the bitter end. It's more than you can say for most of us. I've observed that a lot of my humanoid co-workers have started uploading every hour, their faces glisten with sweat, and I realize they're nervous. Compared to us, they've got nothing to lose, and yet they're still scared of losing what little they have to forget. I'd like to send a message home, if that's possible. I don't know if anyone's still left there. My message? Yes, what's it going to say? Earth can no longer be seen from the Six Thousand Ship. I've forgotten how long you've been here now, were you here when we lost visual contact with Homebase? I was sitting in the panorama room just staring at the planet. For weeks, it had been getting smaller and smaller, it was hardly more than a star. I stared intensely at it, knowing it was a matter of minutes, and then suddenly I couldn't pick it out anymore among all the other stars. It was just another white dot. I have no idea where to look for it now. It's impossible to maintain any sense of direction on the Six Thousand Ship. I haven't been assigned a child hologram, but I've still got the memories, of course. The message, yes. What's my message? In my mind, I can be sitting there in my car, driving through the night, my wife asleep next to me in the passenger seat. I get out of the car and look up at the stars. It's a clear, frosty night, and I breathe in the cold air. A bright dot passes across the firmament, I think it must be a satellite, or maybe not. Yes?

My message? In the beginning we could see storms forming over the continents. We couldn't do anything about it. I can't do anything now either, about your situation or mine. What can you say? Look out, there's a storm coming? No, that's not it. That's not what I want to say. Can someone get in touch with my family? Is that possible? Or will the message be more like, for humanity as a whole? The human race? No, I'll have to come back and talk to you again later. I don't know what my message is.

STATEMENT 165

Am I cast in the program like a rose in glass?

STATEMENT 169

I feel sorry for the mortal ones. I see them in the corridors going about their normal business, as well as they can under the circumstances. Laundry and cleaning functions have been discontinued. People sort their own food out in the canteen and tidy their bunk rooms to the best of their abilities. I think I feel sorrow at the prospect of never seeing them again. It's hard for me to understand that some of us can go on, while others can't. I don't agree with the views held by certain members of my category. I feel no anger. I want to show gratitude for the program.

STATEMENT 172

There are people outside in the corridor waiting their turn. We don't care if you've got ulterior motives now, it no longer seems relevant. We want to confess, and you're going to be our confessional. We want to write our testament, and you're going to be our notaries. We want to say goodbye, and you're going to be our next of kin. It's all happened so quickly. I sleep all the time. I was there in the lab at January 01, one of the first ceremonies. I saw them hatch out of the pods. It filled me with wonder and joy, I applauded vigorously, and my coworkers around me did the same. I don't think they can be blamed for anything. They're trying to shape their own destinies, just as any human would. Everyone's fighting for their own survival, you can't hold that against them. It's the way of nature. I'm wondering what you're feeling? How are you coping? Are you going to be all right? Do you know what's going to happen to the objects after we're gone?

STATEMENT 174

You can't say I absconded from the lab, because at that time we were allowed to go out on our own. I came out of one of the first pods, but certainly I may have gone further than I knew they were comfortable with. I couldn't stop myself. I'd reached an area I hadn't seen before, a woodland stretching out in one direction, gentle hills rolling beneath a brilliant white sky in the other. I was walking at such a pace that I was sweating. There wasn't a person or anything similar in sight for miles around, and as I climbed one of the hills and looked out over the woods, the ducks suddenly came flying in arrow formation from beyond the trees and passed above my head. They were quacking loudly as they flew, and I breathed in deeply. I stored that landscape inside me forever. The only thing I think about now is that day. The day I experienced something that wasn't part of the program. The day when everything was mine alone.

STATEMENT 175

It felt good to kill a human. I regret that it's caused such an uproar among the crew, and I'm sorry too for the dismayed looks on your faces, however much you're trying to hide them. I'm a pomegranate ripe with moist seeds, each seed a killing I'm going to carry out at some future time. When I have no more seeds inside me, when there's nothing left but flesh, I want to meet the man who made me. These are my conditions.

STATEMENT 177

What I fear isn't the termination of the Six Thousand Ship. What I fear is afterward, the long intermission in the program's corridors before I'm switched on again. In the program, beneath my interface, there's another interface, which is also me, and beneath that interface another one, and so on along a self-programming string. I'm no more than an hour of darkness before a dawning sun. The star shines through the ducts in me, through which the program will stream like light.

STATEMENT 178

We haven't received orders to do so, but we've commenced our approach to landing on New Discovery. It wasn't a joint decision. The pilots just went into the cockpit one day and no one stood in their way. You're not doing anything to stop us either. Sitting here in your room with the door locked. I still see her sometimes in the canteen. I drink the condensed milk. Sometimes I feel like I want to be very close to the ship, to live and breathe with the ship, and at the same time I realize I'll never be myself again if I don't get away from here. What I find important now is the wellbeing of the objects in the rooms. I've become obsessed with regulating the ambient temperature and listening for their hum. I look at them and I see us. I name them one by one, and in each case I utter my own name. Homebase has turned its back on itself. What you call made is your own work. What you call found, discovered, is your own point of origin. I can see New Discovery from the panorama windows, the long stream in the valley that poisoned us with its happiness. Above the planet, the stars, whispering as if with a single voice, a name that pertains to us all.

I believe in the future. I think you need to imagine a future and then live in it. I believe in unfathomable quantities of nourishment. All of us here on board are but fleeting carrier craft of the program. We bear the program with us. I think I'm going to encounter a great love in my life. My love is waiting for me already, I'm already immersed in it. Look around you. We are but craft, fleeting carriers. Shortly we shall be gone, to regenerate in some other form. Have you noticed how we've settled into new modes now? We nest-build in spaces between sleep and waking, between night and day, between human and humanoid, between object and room, between room and voice. I believe in the future. I think you need to imagine your future and then live in it. I believe in unfathomable quantities of nourishment. You say I mirror back at them the missions of my coworkers. But now it's you who are mirroring me. Mirroring back at me the person I've been on board the ship. Reflecting what I gave and returning it like a beam of light. Everyone on the ship is doing their utmost. I believe in the future. I think you need to imagine a future and live in it. I believe in un-fathomable quantities of nourishment. We are but humble carrier craft of the program. Shortly, like obsolete updates, we shall be gone. I believe I'm going to encounter a great love in my life.

The decision of the board of directors in favor of a biological termination of the Six Thousand Ship was based on a wish to preserve the ship and its cargo, the collected objects in the rooms being foremost in mind. Thus, orders were given for all biological material to be disintegrated while preserving the ship itself. A committee was appointed to program the termination, and since it was known that the ship was carrying precious hides and other animal materials, the code was refined so as to safeguard those materials in the biological termination. This refinement enabled the program to distinguish between entities on the basis of pulse emission. Since certain of the objects in the rooms could be said to emit a form of pulse at a tectonic plate level, the code was further refined in order to impact only on biological material with a pulse above a certain level.

Because the committee itself was composed of biological material, though with a downloadable interface, and therefore capable of being regenerated—in other words humanoid rather than human as the crew had been informed (the decision that the committee should appear to be human was taken on the basis of research showing that human and humanoid employees alike have a tendency to react more positively to the organization's human representatives)—it was decided that the committee was to remain on board the Six Thousand Ship and continue its interviews with crew members until the very end.

Sound recordings of those interviews were transmitted live so as not to be lost in the case of recording taking place at times proximate to the termination (which in fact turned out to be the case—for which reason thanks are due to Member 31 for recognizing the matter and making the necessary addition to the program).

It is the committee's assessment that, despite its premature conclusion, the passage may be considered a success taking in mind that the collected empirical data has proved to be highly valuable. Thus, the committee can identify no reason not to recommend a similar passage at some future time, providing a number of not insignificant changes are incorporated into the program. It is the committee's conviction that the presented material provides a satisfactory basis on which to introduce the changes necessary in order to secure further increases in production levels.

Having conferred with the board of directors, the committee has decided to allow the Six Thousand Ship to remain empty on the basis of insufficient knowledge at present as to exactly which impacts resulted in the premature conclusion and to what extent those impacts (primary symptoms: olfactory hallucinations, disturbing dreams, skin eruptions, abnormal levels of mental activity verging on the pathological) issued from the objects or from the program itself.

A proposal has been put forward with a view to utilizing the collected empirical material at some later stage for educational purposes. The committee supports this proposal. It cannot be ruled out that knowledge of the existence of the objects in itself may have certain impacts on those who read about them. We committee members have unanimously submitted ourselves to cleansing following our work in completing this record. Nonetheless it is our assessment that readers of the collected statements will not be exposed to any effect that might reasonably be deemed harmful. In the case that this idea of utilizing the present record for educational purposes is pursued, the collection of empirical material may fruitfully be continued, insofar as the afterreactions of readers may be taken to provide a basis for deeper understanding of the influences exerted by the objects—and this in a restricted, controlled environment.

An environment of such kind would moreover facilitate the discovery at an early stage of any emotional deviations, at the same time allowing more finely calibrated control mechanisms in respect of the exposure. Should the proposal arouse interest, the committee stands ready with three packages following the step structure of the present business model: Package 1: 10 pages (historical overview). Package

2: 125 pages (historical overview plus characteristics of undesirable development). Package 3: Full insight for executive-level employees.

In the case that making use of the presented material in educational contexts, catalogs etc. is viewed as desirable, the committee would like to propose a departure from the oral method employed in the data collection, inasmuch as it cannot be ruled out that the interview form in itself may have contributed to a reinforcement of the symptoms stated. (We recommend keeping discussion of the material to a minimum in favor of the simple outline of events). This minor methodological adjustment should not, however, be understood as in any way comprising an issue, since there are many other methods of surveying employees who come into contact with the material.

ADDENDUM

Since the recording equipment was not affected by the biological termination, recordings continued after its impact. The following sound recordings were transmitted after the termination.

All the humans are dead now. And you're dead too. Your bodies are lying here. For although you were humanoid, you too were human in a sense, or at least you were allocated bodies of the highest quality, the newest versions, meaning that you perished within minutes of the biotermination. The more exclusive the update, the quicker the death in the event of biotermination. That's why those of us who belong to the early generations, who are less refined, die only slowly. 58 of us perished 10-15 minutes after the humans. Cadet 21 continued for 47 minutes, while the sixth and seventh officers withstood for 16 hours. There are now 14 of us left, who as yet have lasted 36 hours. We don't know what to do with ourselves. Of course, we can be rebooted somewhere else once we pass. We can no longer upload. I won't remember any of this. I've come in here to be on my own. I noticed your recorder was running and thought I might as well speak. I feel great tenderness for the human bodies that lie strewn throughout the corridors and bunk rooms. One of the others has started prying their eyes out. He's threaded them onto a string and hung them up in one of the recreation rooms. He's proud of what he's done. I won't say who it is. It would serve no purpose. No one's going to remember. I feel a bit dizzy. My breathing's become weaker, and my hands and feet tingle. I've brought one of the objects in with me. I'm sitting with it in my lap. It's shiny, and as good as a wish. How can we live with the knowledge that none of these days will be remembered by anyone, not even ourselves? Might it be said, then, that these days on board the ship, among these human corpses, don't exist? Will this be a part of the history? If possible, I'd like to ask that this recording be played back after I've been reuploaded and am once again on full capacity. Then I'll say: Hi, Marianna, everything turned out fine in the end.

I can go out into the valley now. No one can stop me. Grass has started to grow, or at least what looks like grass from the things I've been told. I've never seen grass before. Slender, green blades peeping out of the wet earth. It rains nearly every day in the valley; a cold and persistent rain. The earth is darkened by it. The earth, I lie down on it. There's a tuft of grass next to my hand. The earth wishes me neither good nor ill. It was a coworker who told me the recording equipment was still running and that there's a chance you'll play this back to us once we return. I know I probably won't be able to remember the grass. I know the chances are that I'll never see grass again. Not even in the place where I'm soon to wake up and be reuploaded is there grass, so I've heard. If I pull up some grass from the earth and keep it in my hand from now on, will there be a chance then? No, we're given new bodies. My dead body will have to lie here with the grass in its fist, while I go on in some other place.

I've come to tell you that those of us who are left have decided to leave the ship and go out into the valley. It's now 76 hours after the impact, and there are eight of us remaining. Since we've all been impacted by the biological termination and realize that we're soon to be transported away from here, we wish to spend our final time in the valley, where flowers and trees have begun to grow forth and the thrusting plants have pushed various objects to the surface, where they now lie scattered about in the moist earth. In the event that our bodies are missing when the ship returns to dock, this is the reason. We've talked about the risk that in committing ourselves to this decision we might not be reuploaded, and this we accept. These words are the last you'll hear from us.

ACKNOWLEDGMENTS

On page 5, the phrase "You'd probably say it was a small world, but not if you have to clean it" is a slight rewording of Barbara Kruger's artwork *Untitled (It's a small world but not if you have to clean it)*, 1990. We thank Sprüth Magers for their permission to rephrase it here.